A SCIENCE FICTION COOKBOOK

And guide to edible niceties

Written and Illustrated by

Nicole Lynn Roach

ISBN 978-0-692-27408-8

www.nlroach.com

Phase 4 Entree

Phase 5 Starch

Phase 6 Bon Appétit

Phase 1   Tonic

Fleets' Fire Roasted Nets

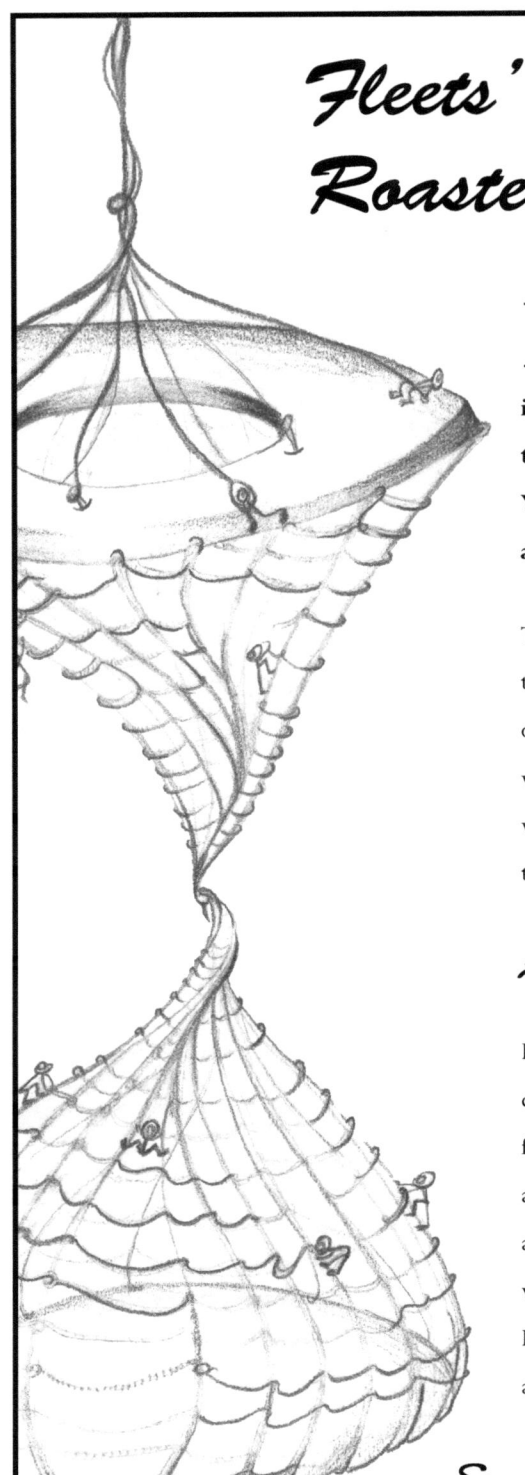

Fleets' nets, are neat nets, and when rightly prepared and ingested, give the temporary ability to understand animal languages. You will be shocked by what some alpacas say about your Qi.

These salty nets dissolve quickly on the tongue and pair well with a dry cool Juice of the Moon, as does any conversation worth having. Tiny bipeds (called Fleets) will weave the raw nets daily if you raise them at home.

About the Fleets

History books say that these little creatures (about an inch high) emerged from the Dunes of Smalldudes centuries ago. Their energy is drawn from both food and sunlight, so they will capitalize on which ever is more plentiful at the time. Fleets will work hardest when well fed and kept near a south facing window.

8

Ingredients

- A Fleet farm
- Plenty of Fleet feed
- Collected nets (to taste)
- Beverage of choice

Fleet feed: Worms and insects in burlap.

Fleets enjoy mostly worms and insects when eating. They will also make use of small aquatics like brine shrimp. Fleets can be noisy and chitter like gerbils.

Methodology

- Suspend your Fleet farm in a kitchen near a south facing window.

- Harvest netting regularly to avoid spoilage.

- Be sure to roast the nets prior to consumption (until crispy).

- Avoid overeating - high concentrations can be toxic.

- Palms may become itchy from handling.

Sauci Lou's Elixir

This Elixir has a pleasantly tart flavor, and becomes a powder when exposed to open air. It is not more or less intoxicating than sugar, but is thought to be a "cleaner" food. Use it to sweeten sparkling water, or in place of baking soda to keep appliances smelling fresh inside.

The vessel (the sphere) is made of a high
performance vitreous material that can
withstand extreme temperatures and
pressures. Leftover spheres can be recycled
or reused. Imagine the possibilities.

Floating spheres and Saucy Lou,

Elixir spheres are good for you.

Use one as a stepping-stone.

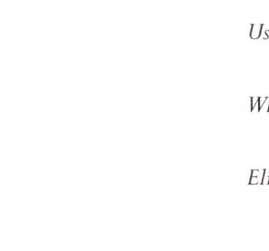

Reach tall branches on your own.

If you are already tall,

Use one as a throwing ball.

Why don't you try something new?

Elixir spheres are good for you.

Juice of the Moon

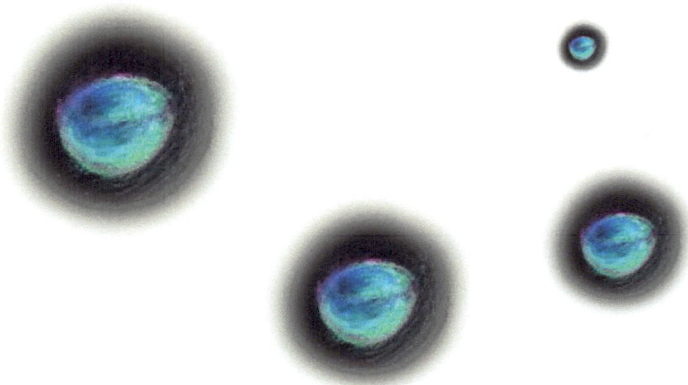

J uice of the Moon moderates body temperature. This tonic will eliminate your need for an overcoat, and is effective for high atmospheric temperatures too. Bring it to parties and wax lyrical about its global sustainability implications.

Juice of the moon should be gathered by a cold blooded, warm hearted, well rested, three footed comrade of the intended imbiber, with an IQ greater than the product of its life expectancy, and a prime number that is below three.

IQ = life expectancy * (prime number < 3)

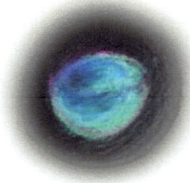

Your comrade will know which moon to collect from, and how to get there, because he has such a high IQ. However he will need a few things from you:

- A ship (for transport)

- A heat source (for cold blooded creatures)

- Recycled Elixir spheres (for juice storage)

More about your comrade: Locomotion is generally accomplished with the two front feet, while the third foot might be used to carry objects (tail will balance the weight). This one is adept in the physical sciences, the martial arts and several foreign languages.

13

Herbal Tea from Humus Hen

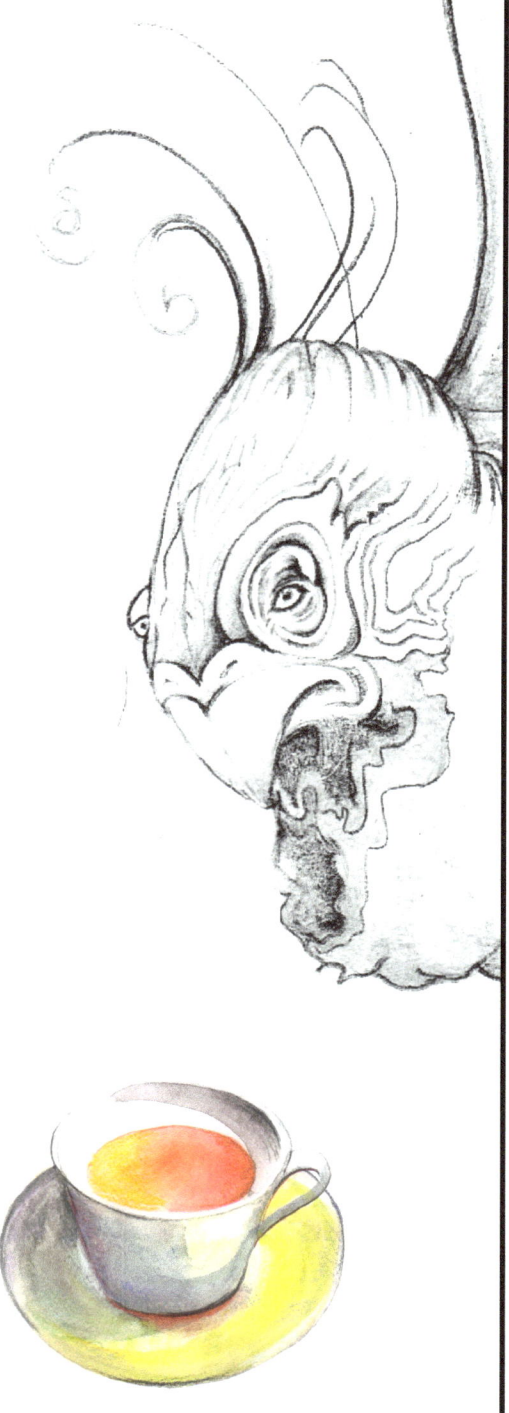

Humus Hen has an operatic song, which rings in the hearts of all targets. Her tea is not an afterthought but a lubricant, if you will.

Effective for jewelry removal, light machinery maintenance, and contact lens soaking, this tea also clears the glide path for your shortbread cookies. You can fry eggs in it, or just drink it straight. Enjoy this perfect storm of culture and chicken whenever practicable.

15

Redundancy Root from the Neuroflower

U se the Redundancy Root to make root stock that is slightly medicinal, and repetitively enjoyable. You will enjoy this rootstock again and again and again and again and again and again and again.

About Redundancy Root

This root anchors the Neuroflower, which thrives in the minds of unenlightened individuals. Simply grab such an individual, shine a light in his or her ear, reach in with tongs and pull the whole plant. You will be doing the host a service, while broadening your culinary horizons... Sort of.

Methodology

- Use the Redundancy Root to make a broth by boiling it in water today for one hour.

- Tomorrow around the same time, boil it for another hour.

- On the following day, boil the broth for another hour.

16

- On the following day, boil the broth for another hour.

- On the day after that, have some broth.

- On the day after that, have some more broth.

- On the day after that, have some broth.

- *Tastes Good*

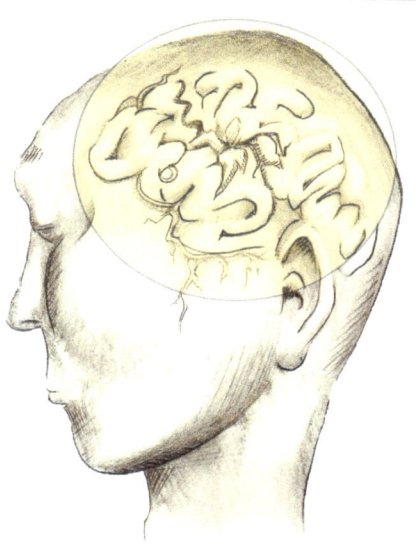

Other Uses

Memory Syrup: Press fronds and petals the old-fashioned way. Collect the syrup in an old crucible and leave it to breathe for two mornings. This syrup couples well with Sweet or Savory Pancakes, as most things do. Consuming it will help you remember.

Establishment: The flower finds its way.

Formula 3: Grind seeds of the Neuroflower into a paste and spread onto a slice of toast. Proceed to think like a flower. Some example flower thoughts:

Overgrowth: This case was not treated early.

"It is dark and my fuel sources are backed up"

"Nitrogen is keen like a morning vitamin"

"Bees are an annoying necessity"

17

Phase 2
Amuse-Bouche

19

Salted Parsimony

A

B

Parsimony anatomy: A)
Dorsal fin and B) Anal fin

Flesh of Parsimony should be enjoyed as a snack, on a rice cracker over cream cheese with mashed young leaves of a willow, and drizzled with well-aged Slither sauce. [1] Moderate consumption at two to three times per week will improve posture. Overconsumption may improve it too much. Other common side effects of consumption are freedom, frivolity, and foraging frankfurters (It's true).

1 Slither sauce was stashed for centuries by pirates while breaching the fiord. Sauce lies beneath a trap door hidden on the bay floor.

About Parsimony

Free swimming Parsimony live near the Alchemy Woods, beyond the Cliffs of Doubt, within the Bay of Sense. "Parsimony" is a general name applied to the multitude of fishes that live in the bay. To reach the bay, the simplest route is usually the best one. Parsimony are most active at dawn and easily netted by the skilled fisherman.

Methodology

From your fresh catch, remove anal retentive fins. Brine for three hours and chill for another three. That equals six. Filet. Combine ingredients in a logical way. Enjoy two to three times per week. Changes in posture should be monitored until you know how this food affects you. Pomegranate juice should chemically, spiritually, mentally and emotionally compliment the experience.

Parsimony roams in circular homes

Without very much of a plan.

He swims on the wall so without thought at all

He may wind up just where he began.

This fishy might flake with a common mistake

To go forge the less obvious paths.

The result could reveal a spectacular meal

Of the fish, willow, crackers and laughs.

Suggested Ingredients

- 3 Parsimony
- 1 cup brine
- 1 tsp cream cheese
- 7 willow leaves
- 1 jar Slither sauce
- 8 rice crackers
- 1/2 cup pomegranate juice

Gella la Horn De Pajilu

Ingredient Suggestions

- 2 cups of Pajilu gel
- 1 sprig fresh mint
- 2 tbsp sea salt
- 1 slice pumpernickel

The bubbles suspended in this spread support digestion, and lighten the step. Overconsumption may cause uncontrollable giggling.

About Pajilu (Pajilu hornidae)

Pajilu hornidae can be ranched, like cattle. They are strict vegetarians. Gel needs to be extracted daily from the Pajilu horn. To this end, owners can cultivate a loving symbiosis with the beast.

Suspended bubbles: Containing powdered cyclosilicate with trigonal crystal system $CaLi_3Al_6B_3Si_6O_{27}(OH)_3F$ plus CO_2 and $C_2H_4O_2$.

Be mindful of their care. This was seen written on a wall once:

"Treat Paji nice and feed him well. For a sore Paji Lu bore a more bitter gel."

Methodology

- Gel should be obtained around 05:03 each Tuesday (Mountain Time).

- The spigot is nestled behind the horn.

- Spread gently over pumpernickel.

- Add salt and fresh mint.

Vent at the tip
of the horn
is important
for spigot
functionality.

Vicinity of Spigot: Between
the ears just behind the horn.
Shapes and sizes will vary
with the individual.

Chewing Gum from Digladeet

Digladeet's chewing gum has a pungent taste resembling that of a dandelion. It has been known to cause Mirage.

Be sure to grab the right section to avoid the spare tire flavored pieces (unless you're into that sort of thing).

Once you've had enough to eat

Try some gum from Digladeet. But...

Grab a bit and move away.

He might eat you if you stay.

Beware of his venomous wit, and his appetite for the insulted.

24

25

Candy from the Sugar Thrush

 The Sugar Thrush spits hard candies upward and belches. He otherwise does not say or do much.

Predict a perfect parabolic trajectory as the spitting energy dissipates. Position a container directly in his line of fire to catch them.

Interdimensional Pizza

To start your own inter-dimensional pizza trees, the toughest part is collecting the seeds.

Here is the rule: Seeds sewn in dimension X must be collected from a dimension other than X (Y or Z... etc).

Conversely, seeds sewn in dimension Y should originate within a dimension other than Y (Z or X, etc). Look for the seeds in old pizza boxes.

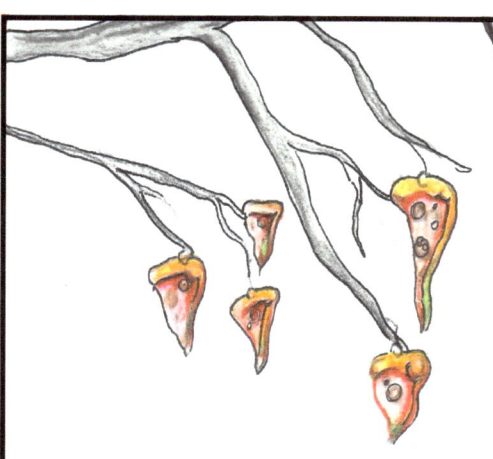

A pizza plant grown in dimension Y using same-dimension ("Y") seeds is undesirable. Expect results like any excessive pizza interbreeding: large sausages devoid of flavor, rubbery crusts and dull cheeses with a bluish cast.

If you encounter your alternate self during your seed search, do both of yourselves a favor and avoid striking up conversation about that scarf you misplaced last January, or that dream you had where your forearms were suddenly tattooed with various images of brass bathroom fixtures. You already know you don't want to discuss it, so try not to let curiosity get the best of you.

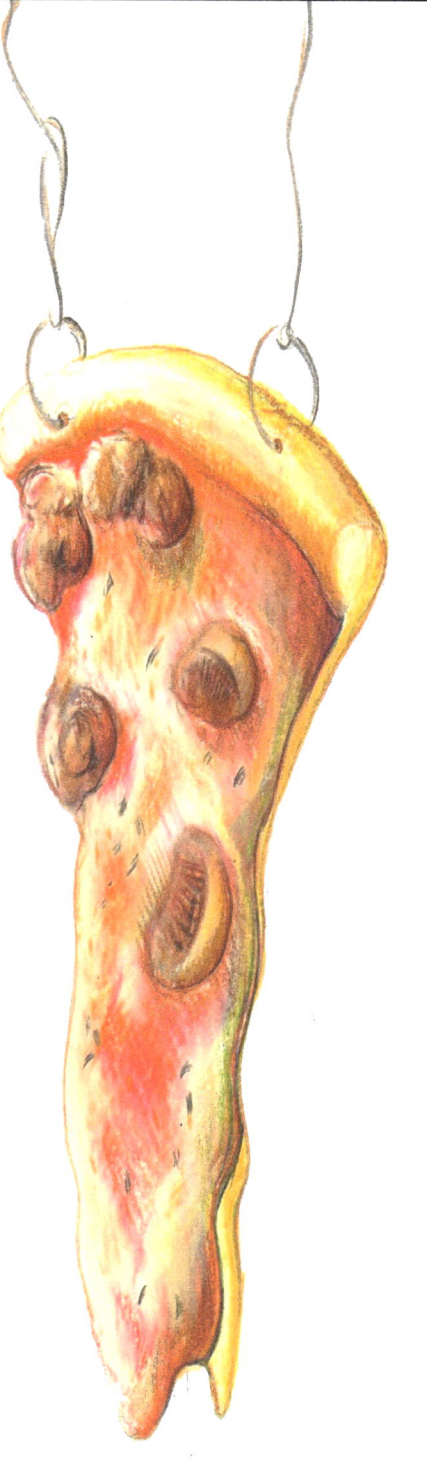

Jerky from Jerky the Gardener

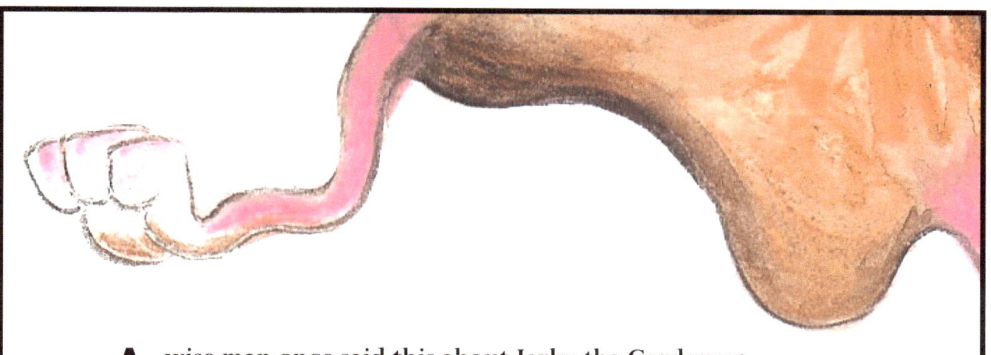

A wise man once said this about Jerky the Gardener:

"He is like jerky. Not him you eat. He is a gardener. He guards that jerky that is like him, but grows from ground."

That probably says it all, but it may be added that one could carpet the average room with Jerky. His menacing presence keeps thieves far away, so his swelling salty treats can reach full maturity prior to harvest.

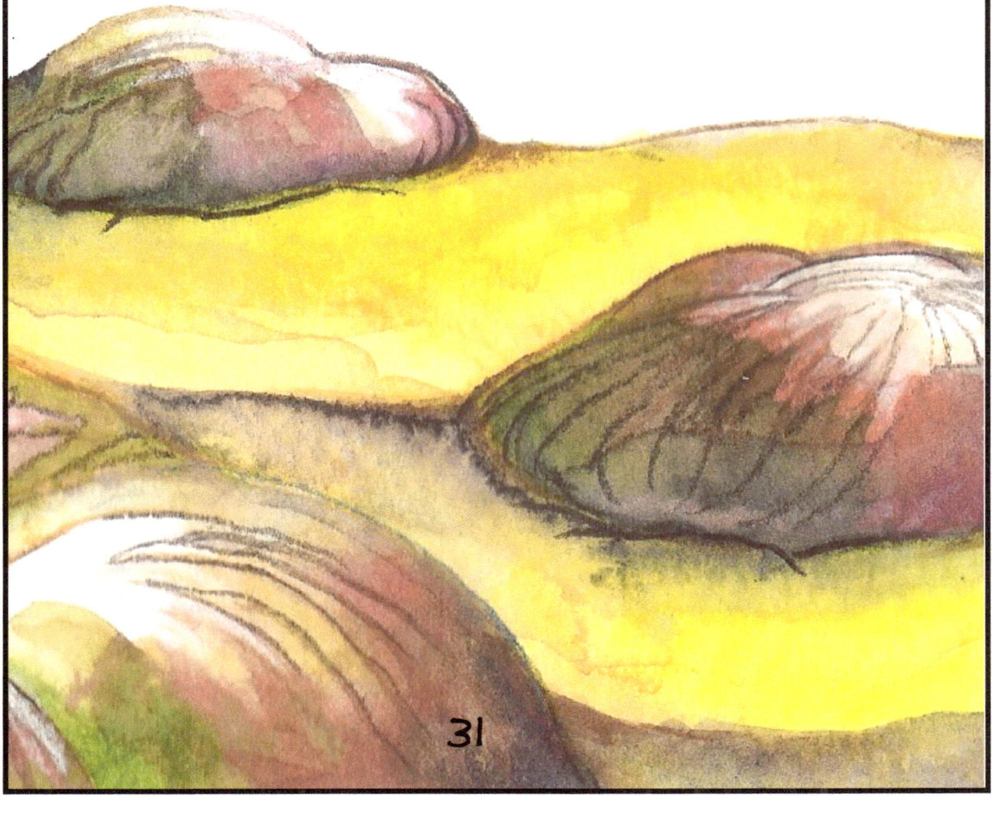

Phase 3
Soup, Soup
and Salad

Doublet Soup

This is a soup that you can learn from. The Doublets present you with a future scenario if you gaze into their "windows". Dine while reflecting on what they've shared. Doublets also love to sing for you in between uses.

Methodology

Boil the Doublets with your soup. High temperatures do not harm them. Serve in a transparent vessel. Remove the Doublets before eating the soup. They can be kept as pets and reused.

"Mal-fated by our bag of rue, ore areas where oxen grew, the queen said hi and fit the life of ox, hog, ape, hot soup and wife. And knee deep in this squid, but twice, for apes and hogs run through the ice..and all the yanking mobs recouped the tilted eye and Doublet Soup. The sons would keep the hogs at bay while oxen roamed where squid would lay. The fern was near with woody coils whilst movies play in cozy soil. A jar was full with gooey rye and true rinks nod to his blue eye. This was the diet and the quiet signal."

34

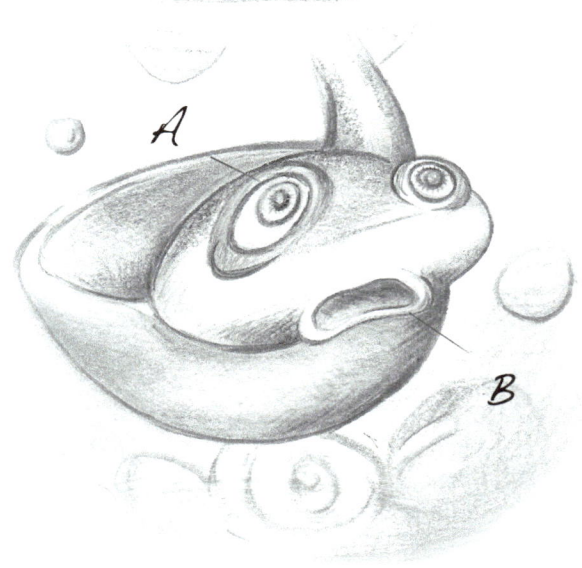

Window (A): Doublets use this for sight when not engaged in clairvoyant activity.

Alternate Orifice (B): For ingestion of meals and singing of songs. A typical Doublet diet consists of collard greens and strawberries. Generally they will not impose on the vegetables that float in your soup.

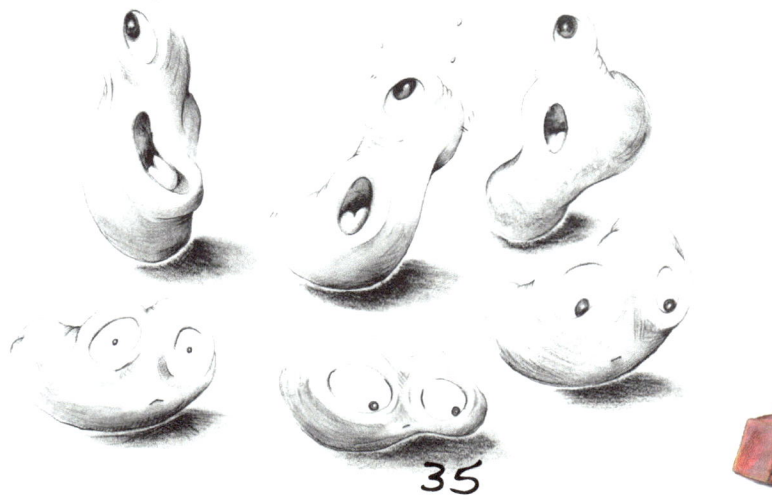

35

Soup Ahorinis
(ah-hor-i-˜nis)

A^{re you soupless?}

Look to the Ahorinis.

They can hear when it's done.

And it cooks itself.

And it heals.

It corrects and lubricates painful joints.

Fetch the soup daily.

But only the pure of heart will be able
to be pure of heart.

This has little to do with the soup.

You can be a real jerk and still eat the
soup.

Moreover what is Christmas like on other planets?

Perhaps the children are all bipedal worm-like antelopes and the presents are giant pots of soup.

Instead of unwrapping, they build festive straws, and take special pills to protect their hard palate rugae from excessive heat.

Salad from Papeli LePhilli

Vegetables added to this salad will shrink in size by fifty to seventy five percent while retaining all nutrients. This is useful for hiking trips and space flights. Shrinkage properties inherent in the Papeli can also support human weight loss. The salad leaves are from the Papeli themselves.

Ingredients

- Spring water
- Sea salt
- Thinly sliced cucumber
- Olive oil

About Papeli

Papeli (LePhilli) are an amphibious vegetable, named after their founder Philly LePhilli of the Fiery Phable Forest Floor.

Rumor has it that Papeli were created in the laboratories of ancient peoples. Other stories suggest that they spawned from interplanetary mud flies.

Their paper-thin bodies will dry out without access to water, and though we

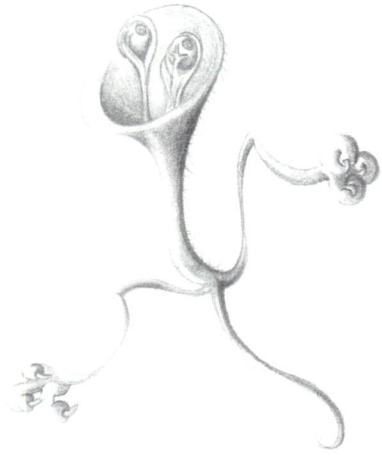

Male

often see a green salad, Papeli can take on a pastel coloring when observed in dim afternoon light.

Papeli are most fertile at birth and also shrink with age. Flavor intensifies over time.

Female

Methodology

After collection, simply store in cool water until ready to serve. Separate captured specimens into bite-size pieces and drizzle olive oil. Salt and pepper to taste.

Young

Phase 4
Entree

Precipus Shank

Delicious and robust, Precipus is usable alone or with soups and stews. Precipus males are by far the best eating, as Precipus females tend to be too tough for their own good.

Know that Precipus dishes were popular in prehistoric Europe as a hair tonic. There is pseudo-archaeological proof of this fact.

About Precipus

Male Precipus will be happiest on your ranch with a variety of other males to socialize with. Precipus will choose a lady mate for procreation only and will otherwise retain bachelor status.

If you are feeling impressed by his magnificence, there is no need to kill to enjoy. Precipus will shed a few limbs each year (usually in the fall and spring), which should be collected promptly and either used or frozen within a day or two.

Ingredients

- 1 6 lb. Precipus shank
- Salt, pepper and a hot flame
- Juice of the carrot
- Garnish of choice

Precipus Shank

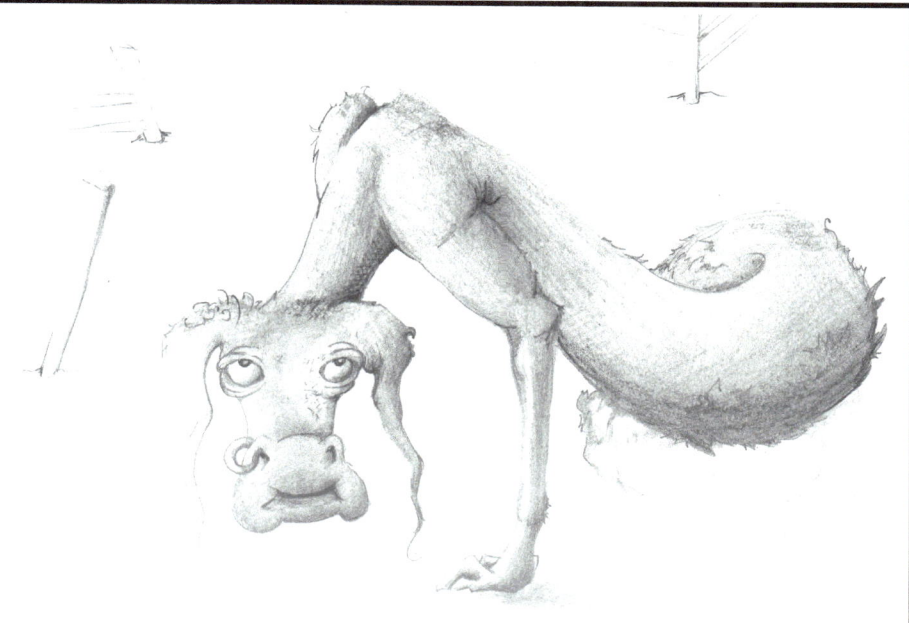

Frequently Asked Questions

*How long until shed limbs regenerate? How do the creatures
get around in the mean time?*

Limb regeneration takes about one week. Whether
male or female, your Precipus will need light assistance
from others during this phase, so it is logical to keep
them in groups. Limbs will grow most rapidly when
the creatures are fed sporeless fern greens and fresh
running water. To prepare, season to taste and sear.
Cook slowly. Serve with your choice of garnish. Carrot
juice provides balance.

Filamentous Opticus Kebab

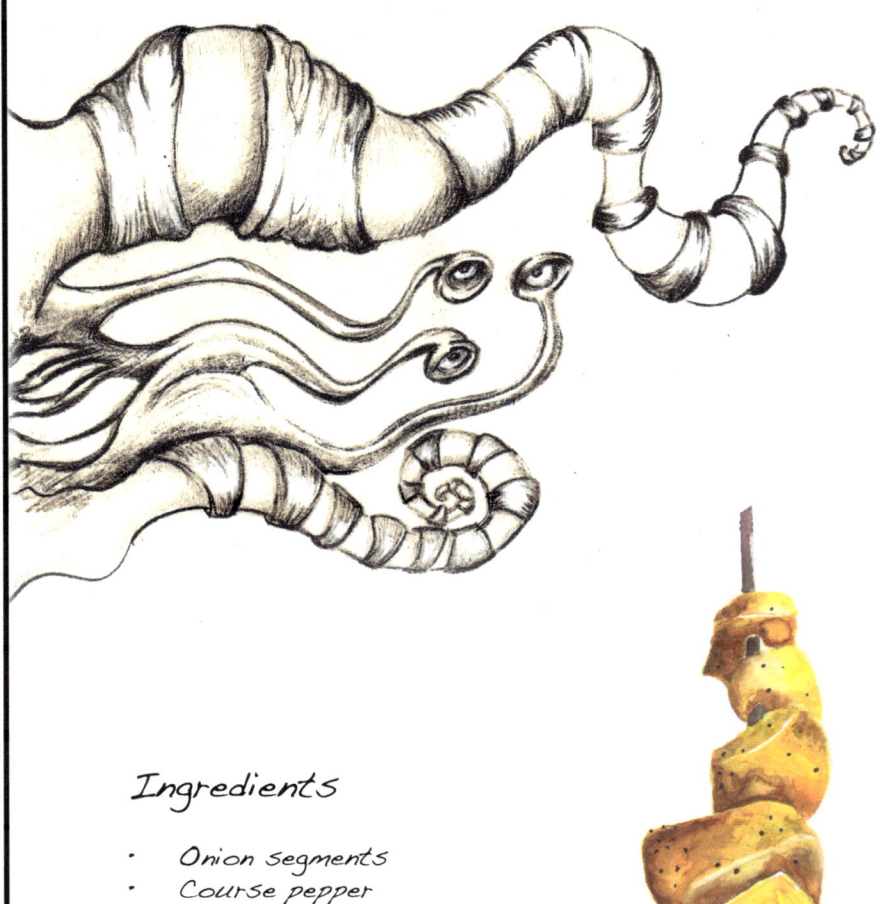

Ingredients

- Onion segments
- Course pepper
- Winter squash
- Spring water

Enjoying Filamentous opticus is akin to enjoying the meat of a serpent, which tastes like chicken.

It contains a sort of white magic, which allows one to move stealthily through bogs and thickets.

Have a skewer, sneak up on other game, and catch them unawares.

About Filamentous opticus

The numerous eyes allow it to see in several directions at once so hunting is the largest challenge here. Some have tried to farm the creature, but this is uncommon because they are also difficult to hold captive.

Use only the trunk of the body for eating. Set eyes and bones aside for donation to your local eye and bone repository. After seasoning with salt and pepper, skewer the meat, squash and onion, and patiently cook them over an open flame. Enzymes in the chosen vegetables will increase potency.

Jimmy Tomatillo's Mean Chili

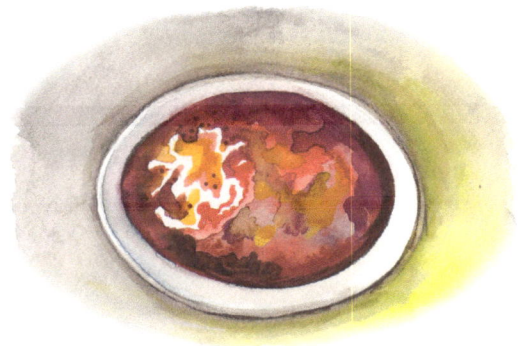

Jimmy Tomatillo reheats a mean bowl of chili, but he will ask you to provide the microwave, and the chili.

Jimmy comes from a long line of vacuum cleaner salesmen who, over time have morphed into quadrupeds. He is a relatively friendly guy, but do not bother asking him for any big favors. Just enjoy his chili and his winning smile.

Eye for a good sucker

Sniffer of deals

Winning Smile

Phase 5
Starch

Sugary Lipid Masses under Bacteriophage Glaze (with Simple Slug Assistance)

Glaze your old broken cookies with special Bacteriophage. They will come to life, and watch over your dinner party for you.

"Put glaze upon them and they'll gaze upon you."

The key participants in this organic conversion are the Bacteriophage itself, and the Simple Slugs. Unlike the unfavorable phenomenon caused by overcooked angler fruits (to be covered later), micronic Bacteriophage transfers a golden aura to your food that keeps your pieces peaceful.

About Bacteriophage

Special Bacteriophage triggers a lively event that no scientist can replicate. The phages will inhibit any baked good, but in this case we use broken, leftover butterscotch holiday cookies, because you didn't really want to eat them anyway.

About the Simple Slugs

Simple Slugs are slippery, yet approachable, amicable, yet fiercely independent.

50

Methodology

Bacteriophage obtainment, although completely worthwhile, is complicated so follow instructions carefully:

From the far end of the galaxy Messier 31, at the fifth star, visit the sixth moon of the seventh planet from center called "Baltimore". Turn left.

Upon arrival, leave a modest heap of your cookie bits out for the Simple Slugs that live there.

Most slugs will not eat the cookie bits. They are far more likely to hoist the bits onto their backs and then, if they prefer it, drag those bits dutifully through the sweet, sweet Bogs of Indecision.

Within the bogs, native Bacteriophage will populate (or glaze) your cookie bits. This brings the cookies New Life, and Hours of fun await you.

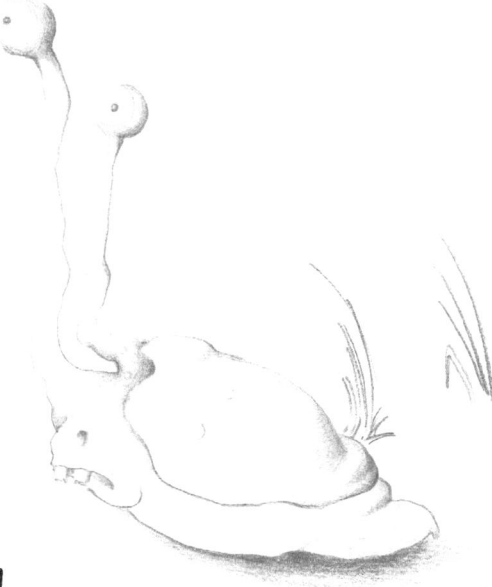

Bogs of Indecision contain these strong slugs

They're a dutiful admirable lot.

They can move through the peat upon only one feet

The slugs put one foot down, or do not.

Muffins from the Bleek Release

Muffin Ingredients

- 6 Pulverized truffles
- 1 cup Nanny goat milk
- 1 oz. dark chocolate
- 2 oz. white almond
- 1/2 oz. red fudge
- 1 honeycomb
- 3 quail eggs
- Citrus juice
- Solstice extract
- Xenon alloy

Muffins from the Bleek Release motivate the consumer to create large pieces of artwork, or to build machinery with many moving parts. Eye color change and modest growth of the ears are the most common side effects.

Special tools

- Cast iron spade
- Silver Truffle net
- Cinnamon flavored chewing gum

About Mister Bleek

Mister Bleek, and others like him, release Truffles into the woods at night.

Methods

To make special muffins, collect up to seven Bleek Truffle releases beneath a waning gibbous. Offer cinnamon-flavored chewing gum in exchange.

Cast iron spade keeps Truffles pristine.

Silver Truffle net keeps Truffles safe.

Compensatory chewing gum keeps you (the collector) safe.

Honey Bleek

Walter Bleek

Cousin Bleek

53

Toastie the Horse and his Toasty Toasty Toast

You don't need a toaster because Toastie is your guy!

He's on his rears he's near the Sears he'll toast it on the fly!

Toastie is a skilled young Chicago minimalist who claims to love the crappy things in life, but his toast is comparable to toast from the most masterful of master chefs.

Toastie has an obscure burrow adjacent to the sewer systems that lie beneath his fair city. He dwells west of the tallest tower where the view is great but the crowds are thinner, like his superthin aerodynamic toast.

55

Savory and Sweet Pancake Stack

Now if you could be a food, you might want to be a pancake. **They are soft, even, and balanced, and everyone understands them.** You might also live on the Pancake Planet, which is 96% ocean. The sparse terrain is divided into two states: one inhabited by the sweet cakes, and the other by the savory.

Ingredients

- 4 Savory Pancakes
- 4 Sweet Pancakes
- 1 thimbleful of surreal toppings

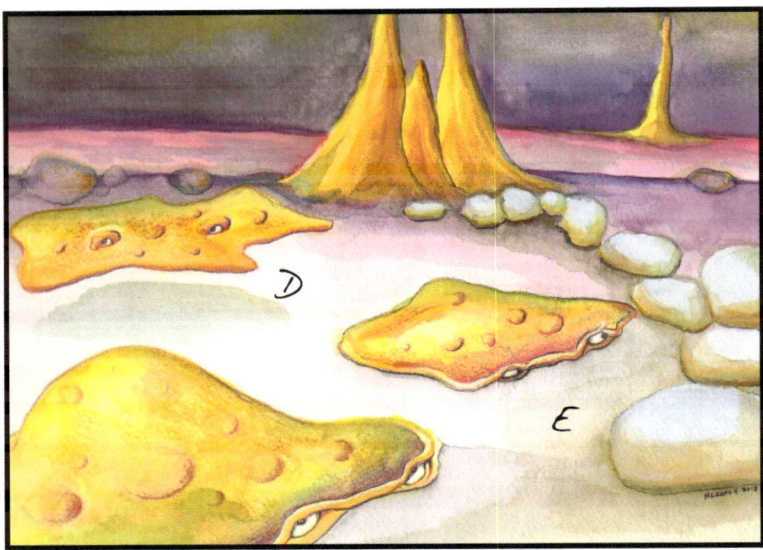

A rare occasion where the two races dwell together:
The Sweet Pancake (D) will be found floating or hovering, with oculars located at the top of the body. The Savory Pancake (E) will generally crawl or "sneak", with oculars located toward the front of the body.

The rainfall is pink there, the climate marine, and there are only three seasons per year. More intelligent cakes use syrup to interfere with orbital revolution, which eliminates winter from the calendar.

Savory pancakes are feisty and speak mostly when spoken to. If they do speak on their own, it is usually in protest. They drink Sanka and read the New York Times.

Sweet pancakes on the other hand, just float around looking porous... and murmur short phrases like "love scallops" and "flair tube".

When the two races interbreed, offspring are mostly sterile. Mule cakes, as some call them, are regarded in our peripheral lands as "peasant food".

There is no need to remove the eyes or the teeth. Texture is comparable to the exoskeleton of a soft-shell crab, or a popped kernel of popcorn.

Savory Pancake, underside view: A) Ocular Nerve B) For Breathing C) Teeth Inside

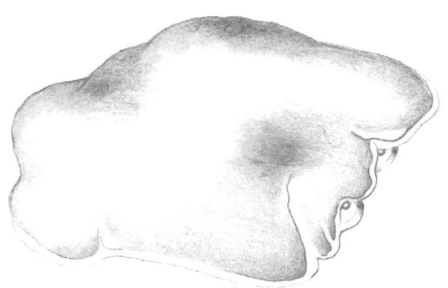

Remove nothing: All parts are chewable once cooked.

Ribitski's Pastries

R ibitski's vegetable pastry will give you patience, keep you warm, and relieve your burning eyes if slicing onions or watching reality television.

And what of Ribitski?

Patiently he waits for his green vegetables to grow.

Famished and fatigued he conjures sixty lumps of dough.

He loads them up with onion skins, beet, carrot and fish roe.

He shares them with his friends the purple woolies: Buzz and Indigo.

Methodology

Combine ingredients, evenly proportioned, in a clay pot at dusk and cook on low until sunrise. Enjoy for breakfast.

Ingredients

- 1 lump of earthy flour
- 1 ladle of muddy water
- 1 paw full of red onionskins
- 1 pinch roe of salmon
- Available root vegetables
- Love

59

Gustave's Stiff Porridge

G ustave enjoys suspension of the hindquarters, and a good stiff porridge. Here are the ingredients:

*Lemon

*Mutton

*Quinoa

*Angler fruit seeds

* Drool

About Gustave

One could call Gus the "loner type". He is also a gentle giant: misunderstood, but trustworthy, misguided, but kind hearted. You will grow to love Gustave, but might find it tricky to sell his virtues to others. Have some of his high viscosity porridge.

Angler Fruit Cake

Consumption of Angler Fruit Cake has been known to help fight off animal borne disease, and to also prevent certain types of motion sickness. Collect angler fruit from healthy angler trees, which are usually found on the asteroids orbiting mini planet Shurli.

You will know the fruits are ripe if they smell of cedar.

Ingredients

- 6 coveted angler fruits
- 2 oz. citron peel
- 3 wild turkey eggs
- 1/2 cup dried currants
- 4 golden raisins

Methodology / Words of Caution

Pulverize and combine ingredients. Bake carefully at 425°F for no more than 3.2898680 hours, and preferably no less than 3.3518484.

Secure small pets and children while preparing this dessert. As alluded to during the Bacteriophage discussion, unfavorable rearrangement of amino acids within this cake batter begets a spontaneous abiogenesis event so AVOID OVER COOKING.

Overcooking of the angler fruits can result in Mutated Anger Cake.

About Mutated Anger Cake

When overcooking occurs, fangs, legs and a short temper will quickly materialize. The cake is far less edible in this case, and tricky to dispose of.

If you get a jumper, it is suggested that you barricade all entrances and exits while it expends its energy sources.

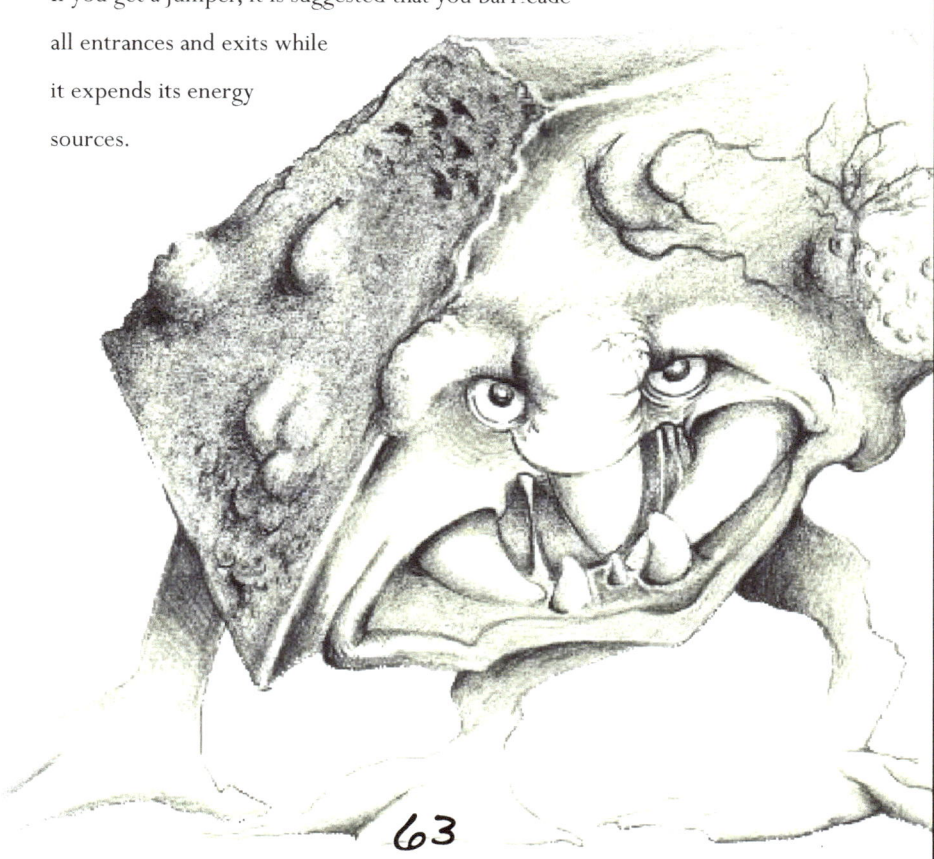

Phase 6
Bon Appétit

The Purple Woolies

Create a scarf from their fine purple wool to stimulate appetite or counteract intoxication. Consider this lone inedible a window to possibilities in the "fictional textile" or "fictional weaving" arena.

About the Purple Woolies

They are a feisty bunch, known for their skill at playing cards and hunting rabbits. Young Ribitski represents the only type of rabbit strong enough to coexist with them, and it all began in the picture above. If you brush the woolies they will nearly double in size.

Methodology

Weaving skills are beyond the scope of this book, but one might consult the Fleets.

Thanks to Abby, Doug, Ian, Joe, Paul,

Robert and Steph for inspiring or

supporting, or both.